A Visit from Saint Nicholas

A Visit from Saint Nicholas

Clement C. Moore

with an introduction by Sara S. Hodson

Reproduced in facsimile from a Huntington Library manuscript
and from an 1869 children's book in the Huntington collection

The Huntington Library ❦ San Marino, California

Library of Congress Cataloging-in Publication Data

Moore, Clement Clarke, 1779–1863
    [Night before Christmas]
    A Visit from Saint Nicholas / Clement C. Moore.
        p. cm.
"Reproduced in facsimile from a Huntington Library manuscript and published with a facsimile of an 1869 children's book in the Huntington collection."

ISBN 0-87328-171-3

1. Children's poetry. American .   2. Moore. Clement Clarke, 1779–1863—Facsimiles.   3. Manuscripts, American—Facsimiles.   4. Santa Claus—Juvenile poetry .   5. Christmas—Juvenile poetry .   I. Title.

PS2429.M5N5   1998c
811'.2—dc21   97–40730
                                                        CIP

Huntington Library Press

1151 Oxford Road • San Marino, CA 91108

A Christmas Keepsake from the Huntington Library Press

 We celebrate the year's most joyous holiday with this special edition of A *Visit from Saint Nicholas*, the first to reproduce a manuscript of the poem and an early printed edition of it, both in the collection of the Huntington Library.

The introduction is followed immediately by facsimiles of the manuscript and then the book, without page numbers, as in the original.

The author of "A Visit from Saint Nicholas," Clement Clarke Moore (1779–1863), was a scholar and teacher of Hebrew and Greek as well as a gifted amateur architect and musician. The poem was written in December 1822, presumably intended just for his family. However, an enthusiastic houseguest later sent a copy anonymously to Orville L. Holley, the editor of the Troy, New York, *Sentinel*, where it was first published on December 23, 1823. Tradition holds that Moore was chagrined by the publication of verses meant just for his children, but the immensely popular poem was reprinted annually thereafter. It was not until 1838, when the poem appeared in the Christmas issue of the *Troy Budget*, that its authorship was publicly acknowledged.

People everywhere embraced Moore's poem, and it is through the offices of one of his many fans that the Huntington Library's manuscript of the poem came into being, for it was obligingly sent by Moore in March 1856 to an autograph seeker named Oscar T. Keeling. This "fair copy" manuscript (that is, not a draft, but copied out by the author after its composition), reproduced here in facsimile, was formerly owned by collector William K. Bixby, a sizable part of whose library was purchased by Henry Huntington in 1918. Moore's cover letter to Keeling became separated from the manuscript poem long before Huntington's purchase, and it resides now in the collections of the New York Public Library. No manuscript of the poem in Moore's hand survives from 1822. There are just three autograph fair copies extant, including the Huntington's, each copied out by Moore many years after the poem's composition.

The printed version of the poem included here in facsimile was originally issued circa 1869 by McLoughlin Brothers, the foremost American publisher of children's books in the second half of the nineteenth century and the first to use color illustrations in those books. The volume boasts charming illustrations by an anonymous artist whose work perfectly captures the merry good humor of Moore's story. The poem's familiar elements are all present, with a single intriguing exception: one word has been altered from other editions, presenting ten (rather than eight) tiny reindeer. It is tempting to speculate that the change was made to accommodate the accompanying picture, in which the artist may have been carried away with the visual sweep of the ten reindeer in his design—all of the volume's other sleigh drawings contain just the customary eight reindeer.

Moore's verses are the unique creation of his own imagination, but they also show the influence of several Christmas traditions that were developing in the early part of the nineteenth century. In 1809 his fellow New Yorker, Washington Irving, published his comic work, *A History of New York, From the Beginning of the World to the End of the Dutch Dynasty, by Diedrich Knickerbocker*. This book satirized pedantic historians and literary classics, but, importantly for Moore, it also contained a number of Christmas references, including a representation of Saint Nicholas. For Irving, this figure was the then-familiar patron saint of New Amsterdam, who appeared in a broad-brimmed hat and smoked a long pipe.

A second work that must have influenced Moore was an illustrated poem published as a broadside in 1810. Commissioned by John Pintard, a prominent merchant and civic leader, and illustrated by Alexander Anderson, it depicted a tall, slender Saint Nicholas, associated not with Christmas Eve but with December 6, and who, according to the accompanying, somewhat awkward verses, dispensed rewards to the faithful:

> Saint Nicholas, my dear good friend!
> To serve you ever was my end.
> If you will now, me, something give,
> I'll serve you ever while I live.

The Saint Nicholas envisioned by Irving and Pintard was a figure of authority who meted out not only rewards but also punishment, and this image continued to dominate in 1821, in a poem that was the most immediate source for Moore. This anonymous verse appeared in an illustrated book called *The Children's Friend*, and in it, for the first time, Saint Nicholas comes on Christmas Eve, driving a sleigh pulled by just one reindeer:

> Old Santeclaus with much delight
> His reindeer drives this frosty night,
> O'er chimneytops, and tracks of snow,
> To bring his yearly gifts to you.
>
> The steady friend of virtuous youth,
> The friend of duty, and of truth,
> Each Christmas eve he joys to come
> Where love and peace have made their home. . . .
>
> But where I found the children naughty,
> In manners rude, in temper haughty,
> Thankless to parents, liars, swearers,
> Boxers, or cheats, or base tale-bearers,
>
> I left a long, black, birchen rod,
> Such, as the dread command of God
> Directs a Parent's hand to use
> When virtue's path his sons refuse.

Based partly on these sources but with generous contributions from his own rich imagination, Moore's 1822 poem gives us a new, entirely benevolent, and humorous view of Saint Nicholas and his antics, destined to become the definitive image of Christmas for much of the world. In Moore's hands, Saint Nicholas for the first time is a jolly, rotund figure, with twinkling eyes, rosy cheeks, droll mouth, and merry dimples, a tiny elf who arrives by miniature sleigh pulled by eight tiny reindeer, smokes a "stump of a pipe" (not the long pipe of the former Saint Nicholas), and makes his entrance by sliding down the chimney. Throughout the poem, Moore invites the narrator and the reader to be participants in the holiday merriment, to laugh out loud along with the poem's narrator. Indeed, when discovered by the narrator, Santa lays his finger "aside of his nose." This gesture, well known in the late eighteenth and early nineteenth centuries, was the equivalent of our modern-day wink, denoting a shared joke or secret.

Moore's poem evokes vivid visual images, making illustrated editions inevitable. The first such publication appeared in 1848, with illustrations by wood engraver T. C. Boyd, and it was followed by many more. Most notably, Thomas Nast (1840–1902), the best-known editorial cartoonist of nineteenth-century America, illustrated the poem with images of Saint Nicholas that developed Moore's vision into the figure familiar to us today.

In the autograph manuscript and the illustrated edition republished here, as in the scores of versions and editions that have been issued over more than a century and a half, the familiar words and pictures of this timeless poem live on to delight and amuse new generations of Christmas revelers. For all of us, whether young or old, Clement Moore's poem will continue to bring a "Happy Christmas to all, and to all, a good night!"

Sara S. Hodson
Curator of Literary Manuscripts

Suggestions for further reading:

Hearn, Michael Patrick. *McLoughlin Brothers, Publishers* (Los Angeles: Dawson's Book Shop, 1980).

Miles, Clement A. *Christmas in Ritual and Tradition, Christian and Pagan* (London, 1912); reissued as *Christmas Customs and Traditions: Their History and Significance* (New York: Dover Publications, 1976).

Nissenbaum, Stephen. *The Battle for Christmas* (New York: Alfred A. Knopf, 1996).

St. Hill, Thomas Nast. *Thomas Nast's Christmas Drawings for the Human Race* (New York: Harper & Row, 1971).

A Visit from Saint Nicholas

A facsimile of Huntington Library manuscript HM 752

A Visit from St. Nicholas.

'Twas the night before Christmas, when all through the house
Not a creature was stirring, not even a mouse;
The stockings were hung by the chimney with care,
In hopes that St. Nicholas soon would be there;
The children were nestled all snug in their beds,
While visions of sugar-plums danced in their heads;
And Mamma in her 'kerchief, and I in my cap,
Had just settled our brains for a long winter's nap;
When out on the lawn there arose such a clatter,
I sprang from the bed to see what was the matter.
Away to the window I flew like a flash,
Tore open the shutters and threw up the sash.
The moon, on the breast of the new-fallen snow,
Gave the lustre of mid-day to objects below,
When, what to my wondering eyes should appear,
But a miniature sleigh, and eight tiny rein-deer,
With a little old driver, so lively and quick,
I knew in a moment it must be St. Nick.

More rapid than eagles his coursers they came,

And he whistled, and shouted, and called them by name;

"Now, Dasher! now, Dancer! now, Prancer and Vixen!

"On, Comet! on, Cupid! On, Donder and Blitzen!

To the top of the porch! to the top of the wall!

Now dash away! dash away! dash away all!"

As dry leaves that before the wild hurricane fly,

When they meet with an obstacle, mount to the sky;

So up to the house-top the coursers they flew,

With the sleigh full of Toys, and St. Nicholas too.

And then, in a twinkling, I heard on the roof

The prancing and pawing of each little hoof —

As I drew in my head, and was turning around,

Down the chimney St. Nicholas came with a bound.

He was dressed all in fur, from his head to his foot,

And his clothes were all tarnished with ashes and soot;

A bundle of Toys he had flung on his back,

And he look'd like a pedlar just opening his pack.

His eyes—how they twinkled! his dimples how merry!

His cheeks were like roses, his nose like a cherry!

His droll little mouth was drawn up like a bow,
And the beard of his chin was as white as the snow;
The stump of a pipe he held tight in his teeth,
And the smoke it encircled his head like a wreath;
He had a broad face and a round little belly,
That shook when he laughed, like a bowlfull of jelly.
He was chubby and plump, a right jolly old elf,
And I laughed when I saw him, in spite of myself;
A wink of his eye and a twist of his head,
Soon gave me to know I had nothing to dread;
He spoke not a word, but went straight to his work,
And fill'd all the stockings; then turned with a jerk,
And laying his finger aside of his nose,
And giving a nod, up the chimney he rose;
He sprang to his sleigh, to his team gave a whistle,
And away they all flew like the down of a thistle.
But I heard him exclaim, ere he drove out of sight,
"Happy Christmas to all, and to all a good night."

                              Clement C. Moore.

A Visit from Saint Nicholas

A facsimile of Huntington Library rare book 251027

'TWAS the night before Christmas, when all through the house
Not a creature was stirring, not even a mouse;
The stockings were hung by the chimney with care,
In hopes that St. Nicholas soon would be there.
The children were nestled all snug in their beds,
While visions of sugar-plums danced in their heads;

And Mamma in her kerchief and I in my cap,

Had just settled our brains for a long winter's nap—

When out on the lawn there rose such a clatter,

I sprang from my bed to see what was the matter:

Away to the window I flew like a flash,

Tore open the shutters and threw up the sash,

The moon, on the breast of the new-fallen snow,

Gave a luster of mid-day to objects below;

WHEN, WHAT TO MY

ERING EYES SHOULD APPEAR, BUT A MINIATURE SLEIGH, AND TEN TINY REIN-DEER.

With a little old driver, so lively and quick,

I knew in a moment it must be St. Nick.

More rapid than eagles his coursers they came,

And he whistled, and shouted, and called some by name—

"Now, Dasher! now, Dancer! now, Prancer and Vixen!

On! Comet, on! Cupid, on! Dunder and Blitzen

To the top of the porch, to the top of the wall!

Now, dash away, dash away, dash away all!"

As dry leaves that before the wild hurricane fly,

When they meet with an obstacle, mount to the sky,

So, up to the house-top the coursers they flew,

With a sleigh full of toys—and St. Nicholas too.

And then in a twinkling I heard on the roof,

The prancing and pawing of each little hoof;

As I drew in my head, and was turning around,

Down the chimney St. Nicholas came with a bound.

He was dressed all in fur from his head to his foot,

And his clothes were all tarnished with ashes and soot:

A bundle of toys he had flung on his back,

And he looked like a peddler just opening his pack;

His eyes how they twinkled ! his dimples how merry—

His cheeks were like roses, his nose like a cherry ;

His droll little mouth was drawn up like a bow,

And the beard on his chin was as white as the snow !

The stump of a pipe he held tight in his teeth,

And the smoke, it encircled his head like a wreath.

He had a broad face and a little round belly

That shook when he laughed, like a bowl full of jelly.

He was chubby and plump—a right jolly old elf ;

And I laughed when I saw him in spite of myself.

A wink of his eye, and a twist of his head,

Soon gave me to know I had nothing to dread.

He spoke not a word, but went straight to his work,

And filled all the stockings; then turned with a jerk,

And laying his finger aside of his nose,
And giving a nod, up the chimney he rose

He sprang to his sleigh,
　　To his team gave a whistle,
And away they all flew
　　Like the down of a thistle:
But I heard him exclaim,
　　Ere he drove out of sight,
"MERRY CHRISTMAS TO ALL,
　　AND TO ALL A GOOD NIGHT."

A Visit from Saint Nicholas

Designed by Kathleen Thorne-Thomsen
Introduction formatted in Electra in QuarkXPress for Macintosh
Photography by the Huntington Library Imaging Lab
Color separations by Professional Graphics; printed by C S Graphics